Clifford's Fairy Tails

CLIFFORD AND THE BEANSTALK

CLIFFORD CREATED BY **NORMAN BRIDWELL**

WRITTEN BY DAPHNE PENDERGRASS AND ILLUSTRATED BY RÉMY SIMARD

SCHOLASTIC INC.

Scholastic and The Normal Bridwell Trust have worked with a carefully selected author and illustrator to ensure that this book is of the same quality as the original Clifford book series.

Hello. I'm Emily Elizabeth, and this is Clifford, my big red dog. Every night, we cuddle up and my dad tells us a story.

My dad loves making Clifford and me the stars of the story. Tonight we're reading *Jack and the Beanstalk*.

There once was a young girl who went by the name of Jack. Jack didn't have very much money, but she did have a very big red dog named Clifford.

One morning, Jack took Clifford to the market. They wanted to buy some sweets from the candy shop, but first they would need to make some money.

Jack and Clifford did their best tricks for a crowd of townspeople.

Everyone clapped and tossed their coins in Jack's hat, until . . .

Uh-oh.
Clifford rolled onto a nearby farmer's booth and sent everything flying.

Jack had to give the farmer all the money they had earned and they had to help clean up the mess, too. It took the rest of the day, but the farmer was so thankful for Jack and Clifford's help that he gave them a reward: three magic beans!

The farmer told them to plant the beans in the ground. So when they got home, Clifford dug a hole. Jack threw in the beans and watered them, but nothing happened . . . or so they thought.

The next morning, Jack and Clifford awoke to find a huge beanstalk had grown overnight! It was so tall, they couldn't even see the top.

Jack and Clifford wanted to see how high the beanstalk would go, so they decided to climb it. Jack jumped on Clifford's back, and they went up and up and up!

At the top of the beanstalk was a giant castle sitting on a fluffy cloud. Jack and Clifford knocked on the castle door, but no one answered. So they tiptoed through the giant door.

"FUM FI FO FEE? WHO ON EARTH COULD THAT BE?" came a loud, deep voice. Jack was scared, so she dove behind the leg of a giant table. She was small enough to hide . . .

But Clifford was not.

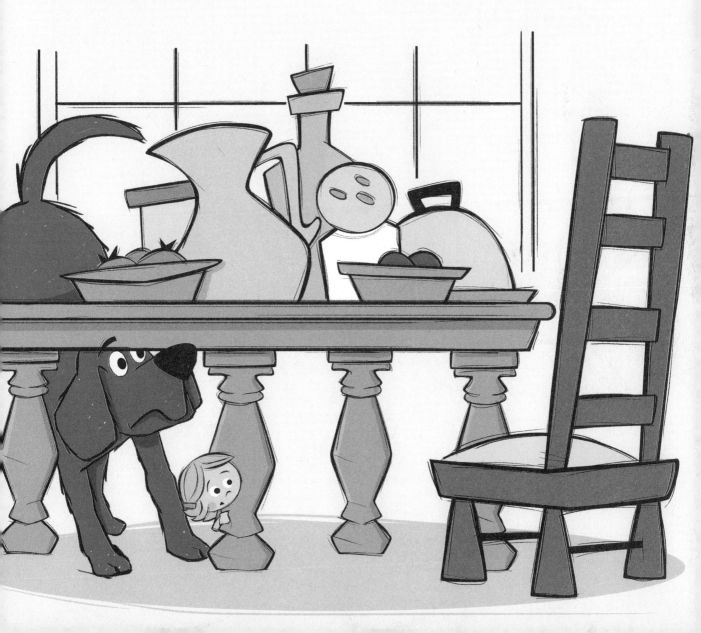

They peeked out to see who was calling out for them.
It turned out, the castle was so giant because it belonged to . . .

GIANTS!

Jack and Clifford held their breaths, but the giants spotted them. Luckily, they liked Clifford. He fit right in!

There were big toys and even a big doggie bed—all the perfect size for a big red dog like Clifford.

The giants treated Clifford and Jack to a grand feast,
and then they showed them all the treasure they had.

There was beautiful jewelry and
fancy clothes and sacks full of
gold.
   Jack and Clifford loved
dressing up like royalty.

The day had been great fun, but before long the sun was setting. Jack pulled on Clifford's collar—it was time for them to go home.

Clifford shook off Jack's tugging. He was too busy playing fetch with the giants.

Jack took off the crown and tried to give the treasure back to the giants, but they insisted she keep it.

The giants didn't want Clifford to leave. They said he was the perfect pet for them and promised they would take good care of him. They told Jack she could have all the treasure she could carry if she let Clifford stay with them.

But all the treasure in the world wasn't worth as much as her best friend. She and Clifford were a team!

Then she looked at Clifford, who was happily chewing on his big bone, snuggled in his big doggy bed. Maybe he would like being a normal-size dog. Living with the giants, he wouldn't have to worry about breaking little things or fitting in the house or eating too much food.

Jack told the giants they could keep the treasure. She just wanted what was best for Clifford. She walked sadly back to the beanstalk.

But before long, she heard a familiar sound . . .

It was Clifford! He didn't want to be a normal-size dog after all!

Jack and Clifford headed for the beanstalk as they heard a thunderous creak—the castle door opened!

"FEE FI FO FUM! WHERE COULD OUR DOG HAVE GONE?" the giants cried. They chased after Clifford and Jack!

Clifford raced as fast as he could down the winding beanstalk. Jack hung onto him with all of her might.

When they got to the bottom, Clifford used his big teeth to bite right through the beanstalk. It tumbled to the ground . . . leaving the giants high in the sky.

Jack gave Clifford a big hug. Her best friend, Clifford, was more valuable than anything else in the whole world.